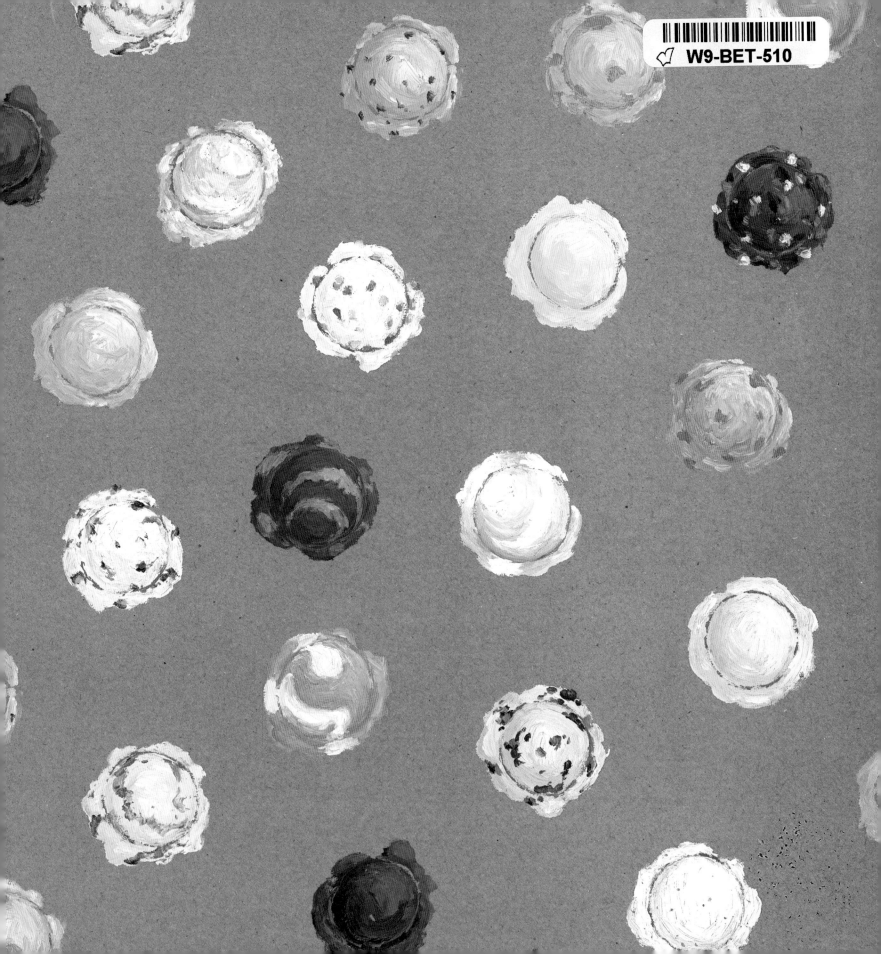

Just One More

Solo Uno Más

Jennifer Hansen Rolli

Traducido por Teresa Mlawer

Viking

An Imprint of Penguin Group (USA)

For Pierce, Greta, and Mia — J.H.R.

VIKING
Published by the Penguin Group
Penguin Group (USA) LLC
375 Hudson Street
New York, New York 10014

USA ✦ Canada ✦ UK ✦ Ireland ✦ Australia ✦ New Zealand ✦ India ✦ South Africa ✦ China
penguin.com
A Penguin Random House Company

First published in the United States of America by Viking, an imprint of Penguin Young Readers Group, 2014

Copyright © 2014 by Jennifer Hansen Rolli

LIBRARY OF CONGRESS CATALOGING-IN-PUBLICATION DATA
Rolli , Jennifer Hansen, author, illustrator.
Just one more / by Jennifer Hansen Rolli.
pages cm
Summary: Little Ruby always wants one more of just about everything until she learns that more is sometimes too much.
ISBN 978-0-670-01563-4 (hardcover)
Special Markets ISBN 978-0-425-28743-9 Not for Resale
[1. Contentment—Fiction.] I. Title.
PZ7.H198248Jus 2014   [E]—dc23   2013034144

Manufactured in China

1   3   5   7   9   10   8   6   4   2

Book design by Nancy Brennan
These illustrations were created using oil paint on craft paper with some digital enchancement.

This Imagination Library edition is published by Penguin Young Readers, a division of Penguin Random House, exclusively for Dolly Parton's Imagination Library, a not-for-profit program designed to inspire a love of reading and learning, sponsored in part by The Dollywood Foundation. Penguin's trade editions of this work are available wherever books are sold.

**Ruby
was always
asking for
just one
more...**

Ruby
siempre
pedía
solo uno
más...

just
one
more
minute

solo un
minuto
más

just
one
more
hair
thingy

solo
un
chisme
más
en el
pelo

just
one
more
sip

solo
un
sorbito
más

and just one more ride.

y solo una vuelta más.

Ahem... Ejem...

just one moment please. solo un momento, por favor.

OK then!

¡Bueno, pues!

Just one more wish

Solo un deseo más

just
one
more
push

solo
un
empujoncito
más

just
one
more
scoop

solo
una
bola
más

...and

uh

...y

¡Ay, ay!

Now Ruby has none.

¡PLAF!

Ahora Ruby no tiene ninguna.

So, Ruby,
how
about
JUST ONE?

A ver, Ruby,

¿qué tal

SOLO UNA?

Just one toy in the tub

Solo un juguete en la bañera

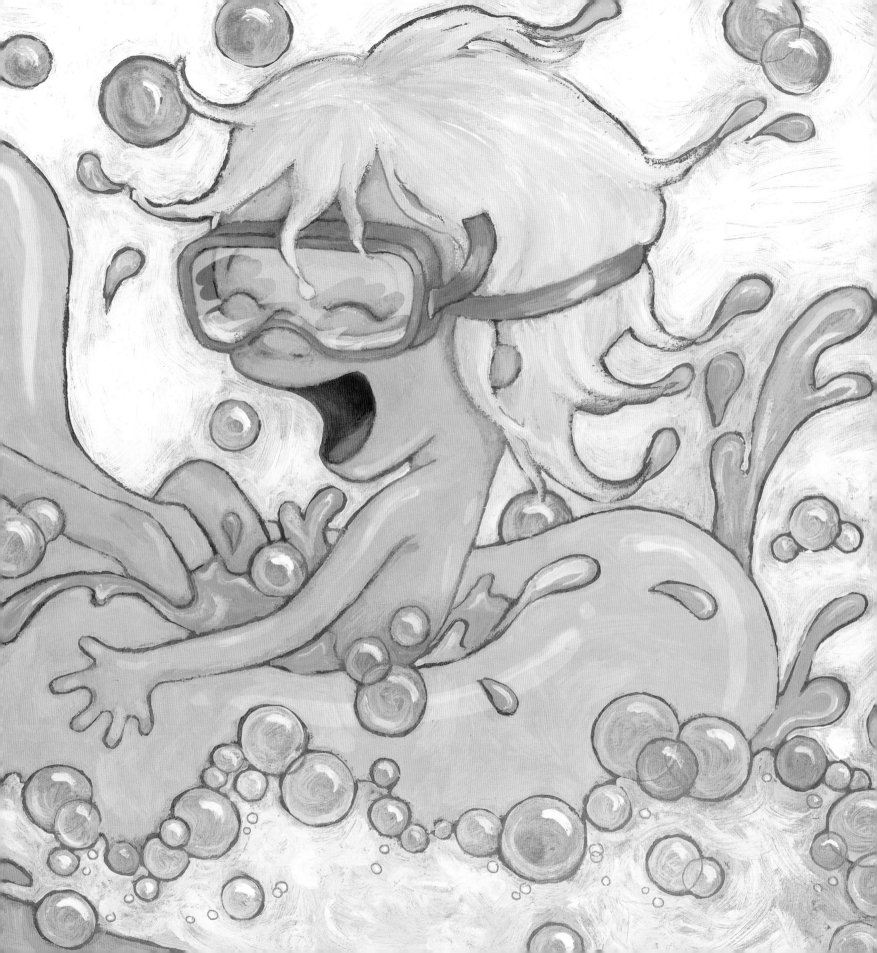

just
one
book
before
bed

solo
un
libro
para
antes
de dormir

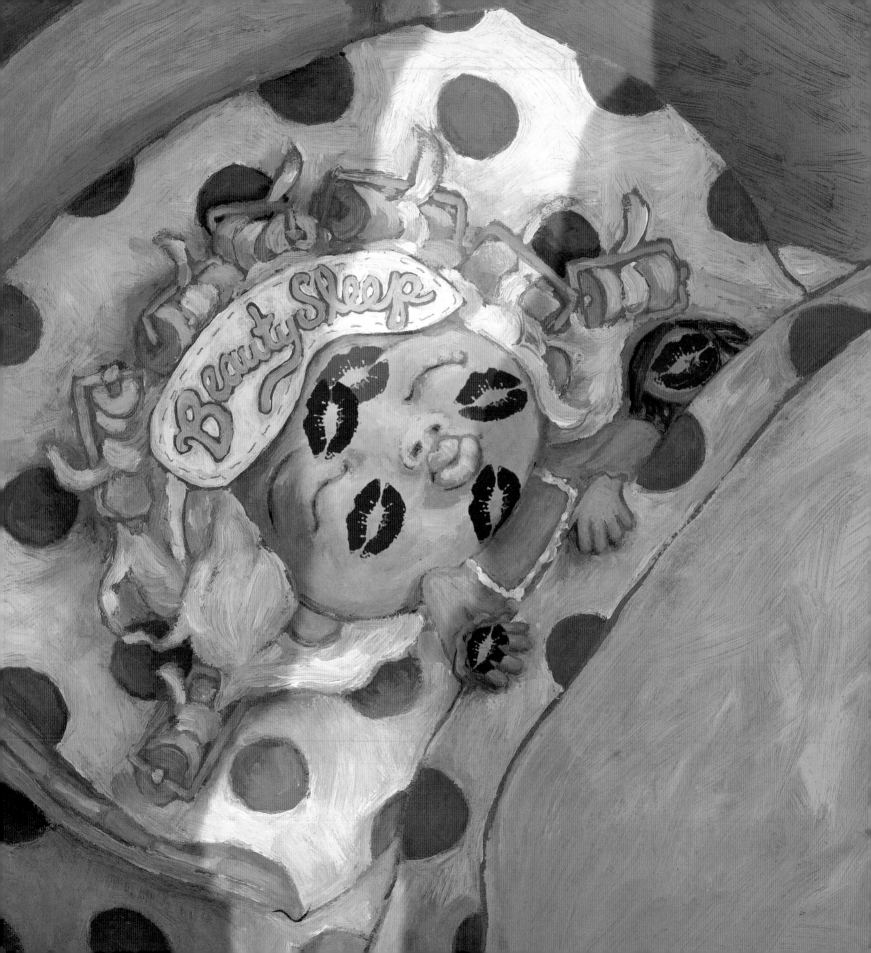

and what's this?

¿y qué es esto?

Just
one
more
kiss?

¿Solo
un
beso
más?

OK, Ruby,

just
one
more.

again!
again!

Bien, Ruby,

solo

uno

más.

¡otro!
¡otro!

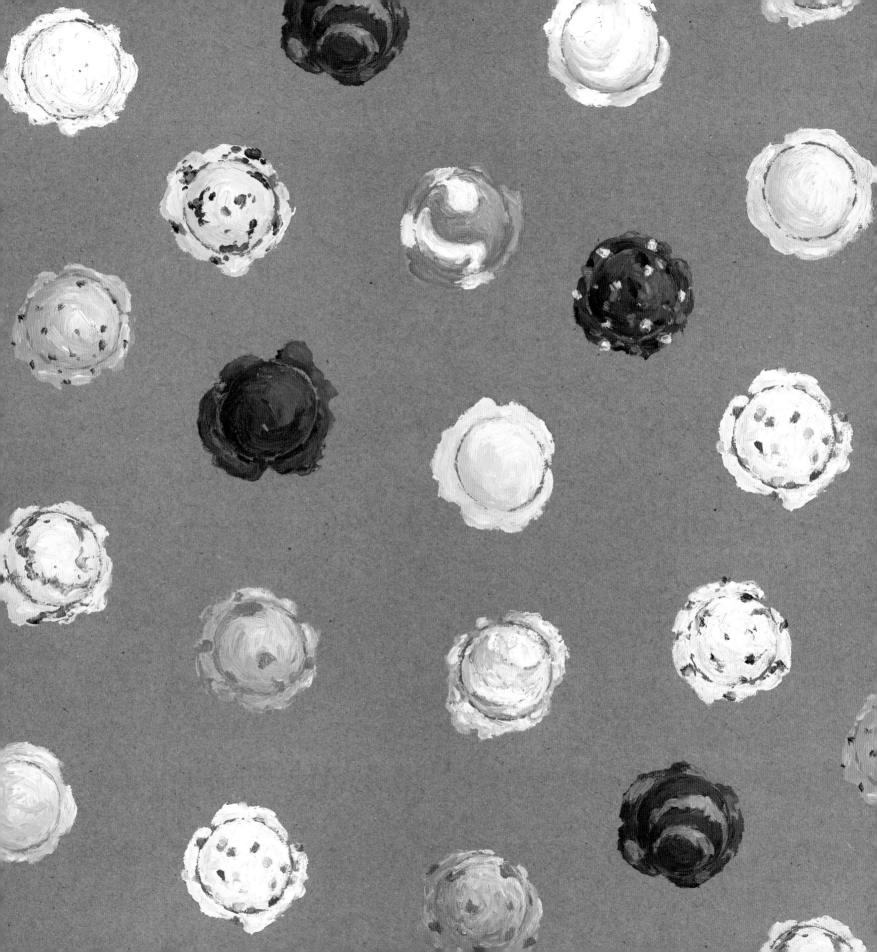

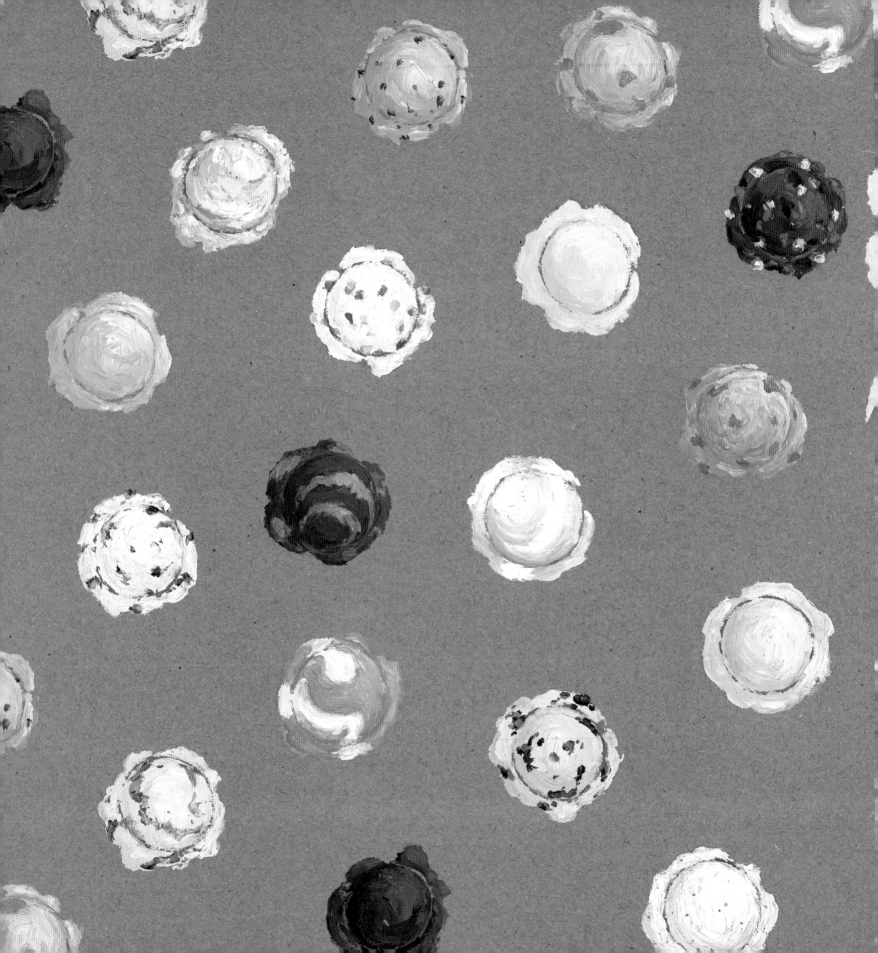